Contents

*B = bronze; S = silver; G = gold; ( ) = the line must be played but cannot be assessed for a Medal.

A Couple of Old Gossips

Paul Harris

Don't tell anyone, but apparently it's moderato ♩ = *c.*90

AB 3022

Menuet

from Sonatina in C

G. Benda arr. Sally Adams

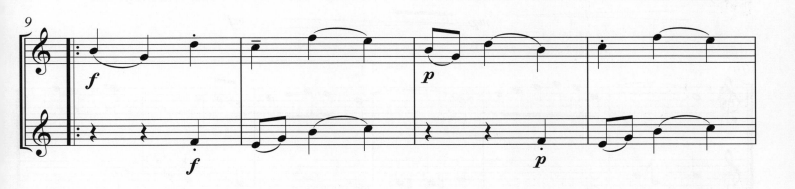

Pond Skaters

Sarah Watts and Paul Harris

AB 3022

Cycle Race

Colin Cowles

AB 3022

Brunch with Beethoven

Paul Harris

AB 3022

The Three Ravens

Trad. English arr. Sally Adams

AB 3022

Land of Hope and Glory

from *Pomp and Circumstance*, Op. 39 No. 1

Elgar arr. Russell Stokes

Straight 8s

Sally Adams

Three Twinkling Stars

Russell Stokes

AB 3022

It's raining outside,
but I'm warm and cosy by the fire!

Paul Harris

AB 3022

A Minute Minuet

Cecilia McDowall

AB 3022

13

Peaceful Pagoda

Sally Adams

AB 3022

A Sunday Stroll for Three

Paul Harris

AB 3022

Country Gardens

Trad. English arr. Alan Haughton

AB 3022

The Crown

James Rae

AB 3022

The Boom-Town Cats

Pam Wedgwood

News Beat

Mark Goddard

AB 3022